BEAUX GESTES

BEAUX GESTES

A Guide to French Body Talk

Laurence Wylie

With Photographs by Rick Stafford

The Undergraduate Press · Cambridge, Massachusetts
E. P. Dutton · New York

Copyright (c) 1977 by The Undergraduate Press
17 South Street, Cambridge, Massachusetts 02138
Library of Congress Catalog Card Number: 77-3054
ISBN: 0-525-06180-0 (cloth); 0-525-03025-5 (paper)

Published simultaneously in Canada
by Clarke, Irwin & Company, Limited
Toronto and Vancouver

10 9 8 7 6 5 4 3 2 1

FIRST EDITION

CONTENTS

For George and Lois

INTRODUCTION

Words ARE SO ESSENTIAL in conversation that we exaggerate their importance and overlook other signals. Many of the implications of the words, the emotions lying behind them, and indeed the dominant tones that provoke our reactions, are not conveyed by words. They are expressed by other channels of communication that make up what Edward Sapir called, "that elaborate and secret code that is written nowhere, known by none, and understood by all." The tone of voice, the use of silence, the tension of the body, the expression of the face, the rhythm of our movements, our use of space, our gestures, and many other signals—some known, some unknown—play a crucial role in communication. We communicate not only with our voices but our entire bodies and the space around them.

Traditional language learning, dominated by a preoccupation with words, syntax, and pronunciation, has all but ignored these other channels of communication. No wonder language students complain that they do not really learn to interact with other people. I have often seen Americans with a superb command of verbal French fail utterly in their attempts to communicate with French people. They simply do not understand the nonverbal messages that reflect a great deal of the culture of a people.

Recently, a spate of books on "body language" has reminded us of our neglect of nonverbal communication. Unfortunately, these books oversimplify the problem, assuring the reader they will at once teach him to "read a person like a book": I make no such claims for *Beaux Gestes.* I deal with only one as-pect of French communication: gestures that some Frenchmen use and that most would recognize. I hope, however, that this book will draw attention to the need to broaden our conception of language learning.

Perhaps there should be a warning on the cover: DANGEROUS! USE ONLY AS DIRECTED! Gesturing may get you into trouble, or at least put you in difficult situations, if you do not know the cultural implications of different gestures. Of course, the same rule applies to words. The expression fellow students tricked me into learning in Poland was *psiakrew* and in Mexico *cabrón.* These words have no shocking connotations when they are translated into English, but "dog blood" and "billy goat" bring conversation to an embarrassing halt in Poland and Mexico. My friends were playing the time-honored game of teasing a foreigner, and I went along with it.

Not all of the gestures in this book are dangerous. Some are useful when words are awkward. For example, your spouse, sitting on the other side of the room at a party, wants to tell you that it is time to leave. In the United States, one usually conveys this message by tilting one's head and rolling one's eyes towards the door. With only their hands, the French can make the equivalent gesture (*On se tire*) more discreetly.

Sometimes it is distance that makes a gesture more appropriate than words: in a dance hall a young man gestures to a girl across a crowded floor to ask her for the next dance. By gesture you ask for a cigarette from someone on the other side of the room. A truck driver replies with an obscene gesture to the facial expression of protest of a driver he has blocked at a stoplight.

Yet gestures, because of their social implications, often reveal far more than the gesturer intended. Upper-class French parents severely reprimand their children for talking with their hands. Recently, my students asked a French visitor what he could tell about two young Frenchmen simply by looking at their nonverbal behavior on a thirty-second sequence of film. His first reaction was that one was of a lower social class than the other because he used his hands and arms more when he talked.

For *les gens bien élevés,* a well-turned witticism is infinitely preferable to a gesture. So intellectuals use fewer gestures than less educated people, upper classes fewer than lower classes, adults fewer than children, women fewer than men, and sober people fewer than drunks. Obscene gestures are largely the domain of boys playing in the schoolyard, young men doing their military service, and older men standing at the bar of a P.M.U. café—but even proper people may resort to gestures in a traffic jam!

Of course, there are some refined gestures, such as kissing a lady's hand, but these, especially, should not be practiced by Americans without training in technique and an understanding of the social implications. What could be more humiliating at tea chez Madame la Marquise than a clumsy lunge at her hand? You might bump her hand with your nose. You might even touch her hand with your lips. And if you blunder into kissing her daughter's hand, you learn later that one simply does not kiss the hand of an unmarried girl.

Harder still is knowing when and how to kiss someone on both cheeks. Do you go first to the right or the left cheek? What tiny facial gesture tells you which way to go so you won't bump noses? Do you imitate those people who kiss not once but two or three times—and sometimes even more? It is better to play safe and be yourself until you learn.

I learned many of the gestures in this book from young French actors at the Jacques Lecoq School in Paris for *Mime—Mouvement—Théâtre,* where I spent the year 1972–73 studying cultural differences in body movement and nonverbal communication. Since everyone in the school was young, I had to learn about student life again. Usually I had lunch with a group of French students and, in order to follow their talk, I had to try to understand modern French student dialect. It was not the vocabulary that was difficult, since one can always memorize vocabulary. My problem was that in their brand of French, words were undeniably less important than body movement, expression, and gesture.

At that time I had the idea of making a simple movie-dictionary of gestures. Seven French students, three women and four men, formed a sort of seminar and we spent hours at a café table making lists and definitions. Within a few days we had well over two hundred gestures. Then we went through the collection and retained those that could be clearly recognized without words and context by most French people, even though they might not use them. My colleague, Alfred Guzzetti, and I turned one of the school's practice rooms into a studio and filmed the seven students acting out the gestures. The result was a film that Guzzetti edited the following year and which we dignified with the title, *Preliminary Repertory of French Gestures.*

One unanticipated benefit of this project was that I was given lessons in making the gestures. At dinner in Paris with some Harvard graduate students, I demonstrated my new accomplishment. Another guest, Jon Randal, Paris correspondent for the Washington *Post,* decided to photograph the students making some of the more dramatic gestures. While his photographer was taking the shots, he photographed me being coached by the students. Later he decided it would be more amusing to use the photos of the American professor rather than those of the French students. His article, opening with a shot of me caught in a wild gesture, was entitled, "What Is This Man's Problem?" The article was widely reproduced and eventually gave the publishers the idea of doing this book.

When we made the film at the Lecoq School the non-French students were naturally intrigued. The Italians were openly contemptuous. *French* gestures? And with an eloquent Italian shrug they dismissed the French. Why, they asked, hadn't I filmed the real thing, *Italian* gestures?

As a matter of fact, despite their reputation, the Italians do not gesture *that* much more than the French. They look more animated because of the manner in which they gesticulate. Their movements characteristically involve the upper, as well as the

x

lower, arm. This manner contrasts with the opposite extreme of the Eastern European Jews who gesture a great deal but with the upper arm tightly hugging the body. The French make less use of the upper arm than the Italians but they do not press it against the ribs.

British gestures? Certainly the British, and perhaps all the people in Northern Europe, have the reputation of being singularly dull in "body talk." The clichéed "stiff upper lip" of the British upper class contributes to this opinion. At the same time, the most celebrated gesture in modern times was Churchill's "V for Victory." As far as I know, British gesture has not been studied.

As for the Americans, Jacques Lecoq pointed out to me that we frequently hold our arms still and move our heads and torsos in rhythm with our words. I noticed this when I was looking at a movie of the Kennedy-Nixon debates. Kennedy's movements were constrained (perhaps because of his bad back?) but Nixon's movements were standard American. He took the traditional stance of American orators and preachers, grasping the sides of the lectern tightly so that his arms were still, and rhythmically coordinating his verbal emphases with his body movement. There was little movement at all in the Carter-Ford debates, which is possibly one of the reasons that people found them boring.

The difference between French and American movement is very obvious. In Paris one can recognize Americans two hundred yards away simply by the way they walk. A Belgian student told me that when he returned home after three months at the Harvard Business School, his father was shocked when he saw his son walk from the plane. "You've become an American," were his first words of greeting. "You bounce when you walk!" An American often walks with swinging arms and a rolling pelvis as though moving through a space unlimited by human or physical obstacles. Jean-Paul Belmondo walked like an "uncivilized" American when he played the tough guy in his first films. In his later "gentleman" films he walked properly: erect, square-shouldered, his arms moving as though the space around him were severely limited. From childhood the French have been told, "Don't drag your feet! Don't swing your arms! Stand up straight! *Ne t'avachis pas!*" A Frenchman who does not conform to these rules is either poorly brought up or has deliberately rejected convention.

At the Lecoq School, I was struck by the contrast between French and American behavior. To do an improvisation a French student first carefully rehearses each detail of his plan in his mind; then he assumes the dignified posture of a statue of a Maréchal surveying the world from the ledge of the Louvre. An American stands loose, a bit hunched, almost in the pose of a ready wrestler, eager for impromptu action, illustrating the very American slogans of the Boy Scouts and the Marines: "Be prepared," "Semper Paratus!" When improvising trees, the French were espaliered pear trees, and the Americans, unpruned apple trees.

Like ideas and words, gestures have a life of their own. They are born; they migrate; they change; and sometimes they disappear entirely. Unfortunately, we know little about the origin, geographical distribution, and history of gestures. Students of modern gesture can use movies, but the body movement of the past is lost. We must learn what we can from art forms depicting the human body and from literary texts describing movement.

Some gestures that are taken for granted as part of our own culture have actually had a long and cosmopolitan career. *Le pied de nez* is a good example. I had thought this was an expression used by small boys in southern Indiana in the first part of the century. Actually folklorists call it the "Shanghai gesture" and have made it the subject of a learned dissertation. It has been commonly used in the western world since at least the sixteenth century. The Germans call it *Die lange Nase,* the French *Le pied de nez,* the British "cocking a snook." The term "Shanghai," incidentally, has nothing to do with China since the gesture is not known in the Orient.

French friends tell me that *Le pied de nez* is no longer used very often, and I thought that in the United States, also, it had lost out to the more forceful Finger. I had assumed that the Finger was modern, but I could not have been more mistaken. It is much older even than the Shanghai gesture. Classicists have shown me passages indicating that Diogenes showed the Finger to Demosthenes, and that Caligula shocked the Romans by presenting his finger rather than his hand to be kissed. In Latin the gesture is known as the *Digitus obscenus* or *Digitus impudicus.* However, we do not know how the ancients held the Finger; vertically, like the Italians and Americans today, or horizontally like the French?

Cultural variations appear in many gestures that are almost universal. A common example is the gesture of waving farewell. In Italy the palm of the hand is held toward the speaker and the fingers make the motion of drawing the departing person back. In Spain the movement is the same, but the hand is held horizontally. In France the palm is frequently held facing the departing person, and the movement of the hand appears to push the departing person on his way. Some scholars think that exposing one's palm indicates surrender; so perhaps the French form of farewell implies a reassurance of nonaggression. Americans are inclined to show the palm also and move the flattened hand from left to right. A Haitian told me of a Florida beauty queen who was invited to participate in a celebration in Port-au-Prince. In the parade she sat atop her float, waving innocently to the crowd, unaware that in Haitian gesture language she was proclaiming, ''Screw you! Screw you!''

This book includes only a few dozen of the hundreds of gestures in the repertory of the French students who coached me. We have chosen those which seem unusual or amusing. You will note that some are by no means uniquely French but all have a French twist to them. The Royal Shaft done by a Frenchman, an Italian, and an American may have a similar meaning, but the facial expression and the movement of the rest of the body give the gesture a cultural style.

Of course, my behavior in the photographs

of this book is incongruous. An elderly Harvard professor should not be making these gestures. No French
professor would let himself be cast in this role, and I certainly did not learn the gestures from my French col-
leagues! But I risk the incongruity because I am not
French and I trust the French will be indulgent. They are
always indulgent to children who are not their own,
and, after all, they know that *les Américains sont de
grands enfants.* Perhaps I should add: *Peut-être
surtout moi!*

BEAUX GESTES

TOUT VA BIEN

Self-Praise and Praise

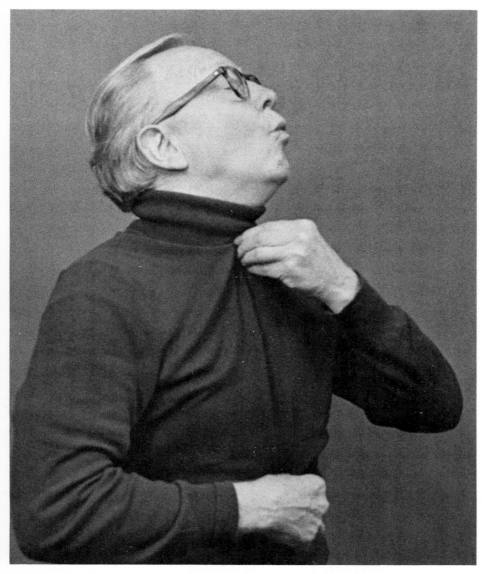

La cravate—The tie: I'm really something!

EVERYTHING'S OK

JUST A GESTURE," people say. Gestures are so simple, so obvious. What is there to say about them? Probably none could be so simple as our first. *J'ai du nez!* is an old French phrase that transfers to man the quality of a good hunting dog able to follow an elusive trail through its sense of smell. A man who "has a good nose" is shrewd. He is able to get to the real source of a problem; no one gets the better of him in a deal. This much we can learn from dictionaries and novels. But we don't know very much about the gesture accompanying the phrase. We know the phrase was used in the sixteenth century, but do not know whether the same gesture has always accompanied it.

Unfortunately, common sense is not always a reliable guide. Take *Mon oeil!,* for example. I assumed that it implied, "I see through your deception; you can't fool me. I have a good eye." A little research turns up quite a different explanation. A wonderful book on Neapolitan and classical gestures by Andrea De Jorio, published in the 1830s, claims that *Mon oeil!* is related to the ancient concept of the "evil eye." When you pull down the skin beneath the eye with the forefinger, you give the impression that your eye is pulled out of place and no longer parallel with the other eye. You squint; you are walleyed. Since the eyes have always been considered the mirror of the soul, any distortion of this mirror raises the suspicion that the soul or person is false. So if you make the gesture *Mon oeil!,* you are implying that someone cannot be trusted. Whether this is the meaning of the gesture today is doubtful, but I have found that the same gesture was used in nineteenth-century Naples and ancient Herculaneum.

1

The gesture made with the thumb and forefinger forming a circle (*Au poil!*), popular in modern advertising, has also been widely used for centuries and may be related to the concept of the "evil eye." Eyepower provides strength. An extra eye in the form of an amulet, or a gesture formed by the finger and thumb, is a source of added protection. In addition, the circle as a perfect form traditionally represented justice.

For foreigners, probably the most characteristic French gesture is *Splendide!,* the holding of the joined tips of the fingers to one's puckered lips, and, with a facial expression of exquisite pleasure, throwing out a kiss. Since *Les plaisirs de la bouche,* eating and drinking, are so essential to the French good life, it is natural that the sensation of exquisite taste should be associated with the mouth.

J'ai du nez!—I have some nose: I have a nose for it.

Les deux doigts dans le nez!—The two fingers up the nose: It's so easy I could do it with my fingers up my nose.

Mon oeil—My eye: You can't fool me!

5

Au poil!—To the hair: Perfect! This gesture is associated with the idea of measuring something perfectly, right down to a hair.

Extra!—Excellent!

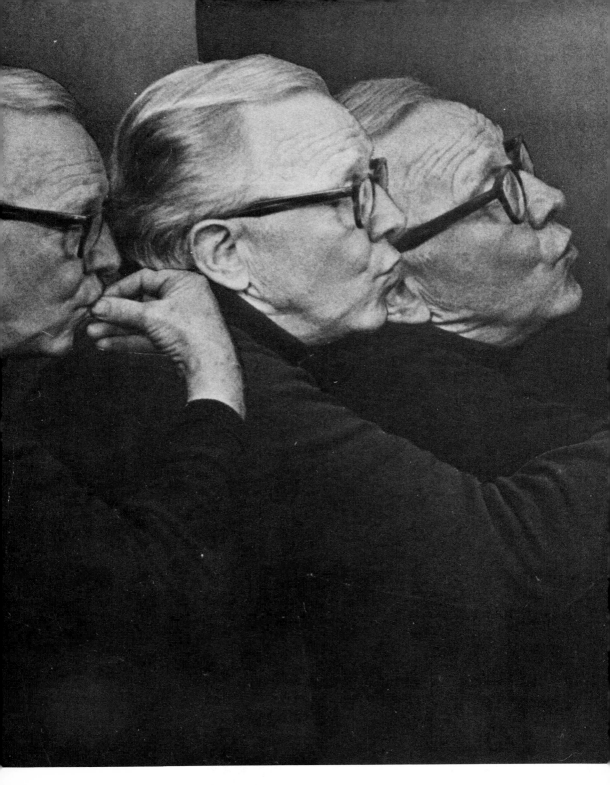

Splendide! Quel bijou!—Splendid! What a jewel!

C'EST LA VIE

Circumstance and Decision

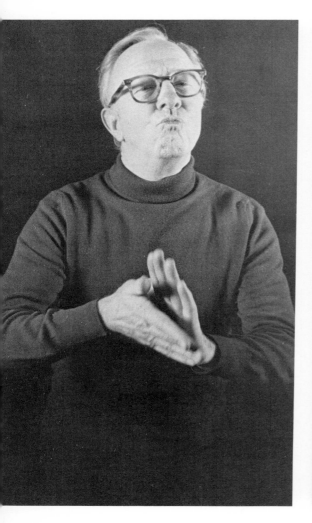 

Je m'en lave les mains!: I wash my hands of it!

THAT'S LIFE FOR YOU

THESE GESTURES are mimed expressions suggesting the need to undertake an inevitable, but not very pleasant, activity. *Le boulot* is the common French slang for "work," though no one knows the derivation. The mimed activity is more comprehensible. Traditionally, men spat on their hands and rubbed them together before picking up an axe or some other heavy tool to begin work.

Ceinture! recalls the need to pull in the belt to give the sensation of tightness around the stomach in order to help one endure the pangs of hunger when supplies are running short.

Ras-le-bol! has been a popular gesture for several generations. However the words labeling the gesture keep changing. The phrase *Ras-le-bol!* appeared during the 1968 "Events of May" in France, when it became the slogan of the striking French students. The previous generation had used the same gesture with the phrase *J'en ai eu assez!* ("I've had enough of it!") I understand that the expression *Ras-le-bol* has become old-fashioned now, although the gesture lives on.

With some variations the gesture that mimes the rubbing of paper money between the thumb and forefinger (*Du fric! Du pognon!*) is common throughout the world. In South America an alternative form consists of moving four fingers back and forth. The gesture also often takes on the added nuance of bribery, especially in the Near East.

The mimed action of smoothing over a surface with the flat of the hand (*Fini!*) seems to indicate the accomplishment of a goal. The gesture is sometimes used to show satisfaction, but it more often implies a command for the cessation of an objectionable activity, meaning "We've had enough of that, you'd better stop."

The gesture labeled *On se tire!* is peculiarly French, but its origin is not clear. Apparently, it shows the interruption of activity by chopping off the hand. In any case, it is a convenient gesture. In case of emergency it can be made violently with a full swing of the arm. Yet it is more often used as a social convenience, done very moderately, almost imperceptibly, so that one can discreetly indicate to a companion that it is time to leave the party.

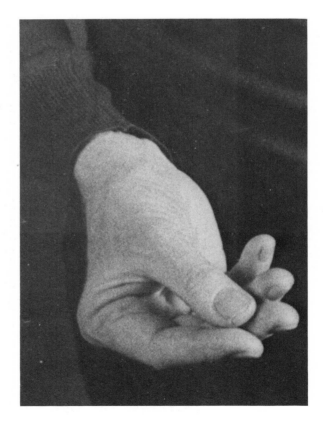

Left: **Du fric! Du pognon!:** Give me money! *Fric* is related to images of food; more particularly, stew. *Pognon* means "fistful."

Right: **Ceinture!:** We'll have to pull in our belts!

(A)

(D)

AU CAFÉ—AT THE CAFE
(A) **J'ai soif**—I'm thirsty: Give me a drink. (B) **Encore du vin**—More wine: Give me another drink. (C) **Du feu, s'il vous plaît**—Light, please. (D) **Vous avez le téléphone?** —Where is the telephone? (E) **L'addition, s'il vous plaît** —The check, please.

14

Au boulot!: Let's get to work.

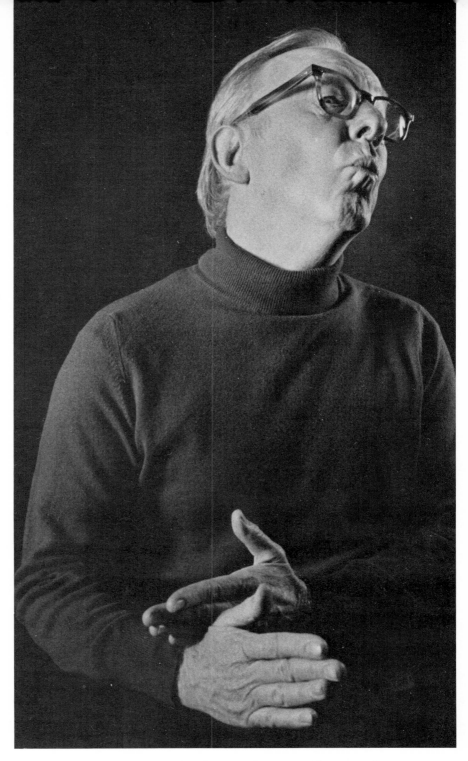

On se tire! On se casse!—One pulls oneself away. One breaks away: Let's get out of here. Let's split.

La sentence!—The sentence: The forefinger presented
sententiously calls for silence so all may hear the important message about to be announced.

18

Ras-le-bol!—The bowl is full to the brim: I've had it up to here!

Fini!: No more of that!

LE JEMENFOUTISME

Boredom, Indecision, and Rejection

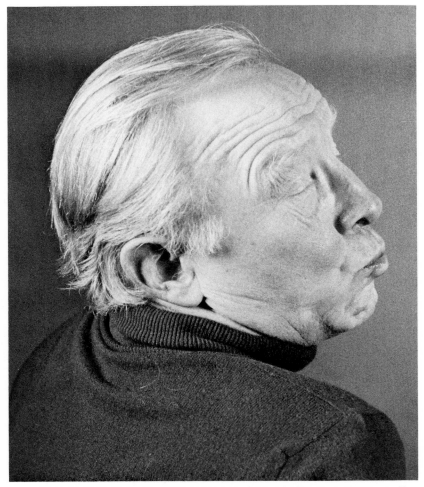

Je m'en fous: I don't give a damn! *Foutre* means "to have intercourse," but it has acquired other meanings. Reflexively, as here, it means "to be indifferent." When this attitude becomes a national lifestyle, as in France, it is dignified as *Le jemenfoutisme.*

WHO CARES?

IT IS INEVITABLE in the land of *Le Jemen-foutisme* that there should be a long list of gestures indicating a rejection of responsibility, the belittling of one's errors, the affectation of indifference. One says *Je m'en fous* with the whole body. A person or a problem or a responsibility is symbolically expelled. The hands are washed clear of responsibility. Responsibility is ejected from the mouth with the thumb or flicked away with the fingers. Above all, it is ejected as a stream of air from the lungs; the shoulders shrug and compress the lungs, while the lips pout as the air is expelled making the sound "bof!"

The writing out of the "bof" sound derives from the comic strips. Cartoonists, who wanted to express the sound of the expelled air, invented the word. Now people imitate the comic strips and actually say "bof!"

Of course many of these gestures are not uniquely French. Several cultures use the symbolic flick of the fingers and washing of the hands. *Que dalle!* is a most venerable gesture. Remember in Shakespeare:

> SAMPSON: Nay, as they dare. I will bite my thumb at them, which is disgrace to them if they bear it.
> ABRAM: Do you bite your thumb at us, sir?
> SAMPSON: I do bite my thumb, sir.
> ABRAM: Do you bite your thumb at us, sir?
> SAMPSON (*aside to Gregory*): Is the law of our side if I say Aye?

23

GREGORY(*aside to Sampson*): No.
SAMPSON: No sir, I do not bite my thumb
at you, sir; but I bite my thumb, sir.
Romeo and Juliet, Act I, scene i, ll. 40–48.

However, the meaning of "biting the thumb" has evolved differently in France where it means "it's worth nothing" rather than "up yours." Perhaps the French version was influenced by the Near Eastern gesture of rubbing the thumb nail across the teeth to signify "I have nothing."

The gesture *Zéro!* is surprisingly close to the gesture *Au poil!* It is the position of the hand and the movement of the fingers that make the difference. For *Zéro!* the ring formed by thumb and finger should be placed directly in front of the eye so that one peers through the circle. *Au poil!* is formed several inches lower and to the right, and the hand moves back and forth to emphasize the idea. The expression of the face should actually be enough to differentiate between the two.

The image of the beard often evokes boredom, as when someone strokes an imaginary beard to imply that gray-bearded professors are dull or to indicate that a joke is old and dull enough to wear a beard. However the French gesture *La barbe! Rasoir!* seems rather to indicate the notion of shaving.

Comme-ci, comme-ça is a beautifully mimed gesture that one associates with the physical balance of two forces or a difficult choice between two almost equal alternatives.

Comme-ci, comme-ça!—Like this, like that: So-so, sort of.

La barbe! Rasoir!: How dull. "Beard! Razor!" acquired the meaning "boring" in the nineteenth century.

Ca n'a pas d'importance—That has no importance: It doesn't matter.

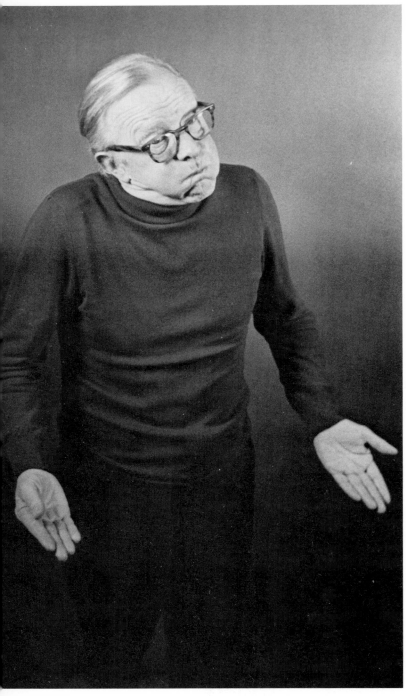

Bof!: It doesn't worry me!

Qu'est-ce que tu veux que j'y fasse?—What do you ex-
pect me to do about it?

***Zéro!*—Worthless!**

Du menu fretin! De la petite bière!: Rubbish! *Du menu fretin* is minute rubbish—worthless, discarded, broken objects. The idea is extended to fish that are too small to keep and people too insignificant to take into consideration. *Petite bière* is beer of low alcoholic content.

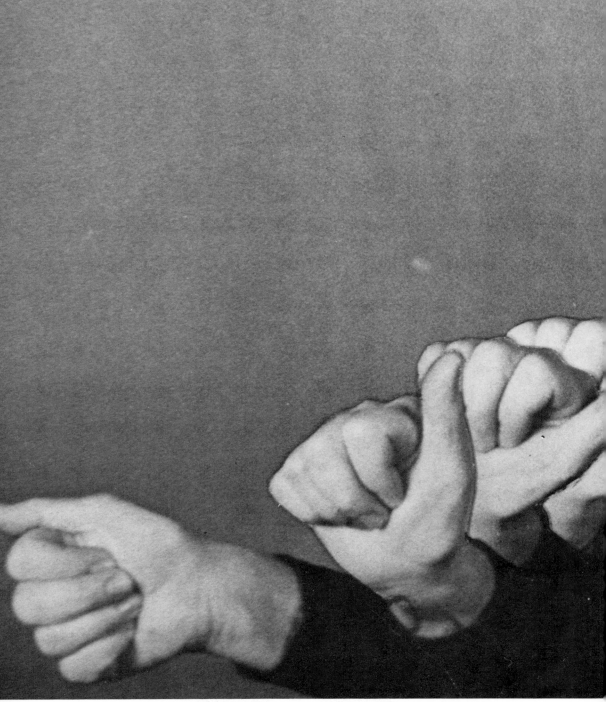

Que dalle!—But nothing: Zero! I bite my thumb at you!
Dalle is a worthless bit of floor tiling, a small coin. Insult
is added through the old gesture of spitting on someone.

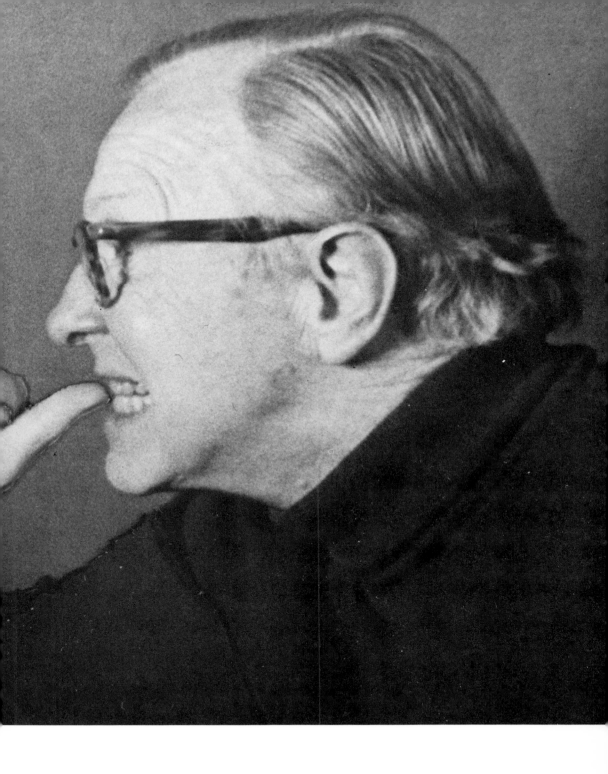

LES PETITES MISERES

Problems and Weaknesses

Coup de fusil—The hand mimes a revolver which is used for suicide after an exorbitant bill has been presented.

WELL, REALLY...!

THESE MIMED GESTURES take us back behind the primitive metaphors with which our speech has evolved. It is appealing to think of someone so lazy that hair can grow on his hand (*Il a un poil dans la main!*). An object passing under the nostrils is a picturesque way of implying a missed opportunity. *Les oeillères!* is a good example of the long life of a gesture. Few people today have seen a horse wearing blinders yet the movement showing the piece of harness is still used as a metaphor.

This category, which deals with the petty weaknesses of humanity, could easily be used to analyze the French value system. The last three gestures in the section bring out one facet of French civilization: the emphasis on the brain as the ultimate source of rational behavior in man. I do not believe that the French are more rational than other people, but they certainly have the most exaggerated concern for man's reason. All sorts of hand and finger movements around the top of the head serve to call attention to the malfunctioning of someone's brain. Indeed these gestures are often directed against oneself—"How could I have been so stupid??!!" The expression is often accompanied by a violent striking of the palms or fists against one's head that is quite masochistic.

There is an infinite variety of gestures to remind an individual that he has failed to live up to human standards (French standards, that is) for rational behavior. The irony is that the person who makes the accusing gesture is often acting as irrationally as the person he accuses.

Three versions of **Marrant!**—Funny!: You may think you're funny but you aren't.

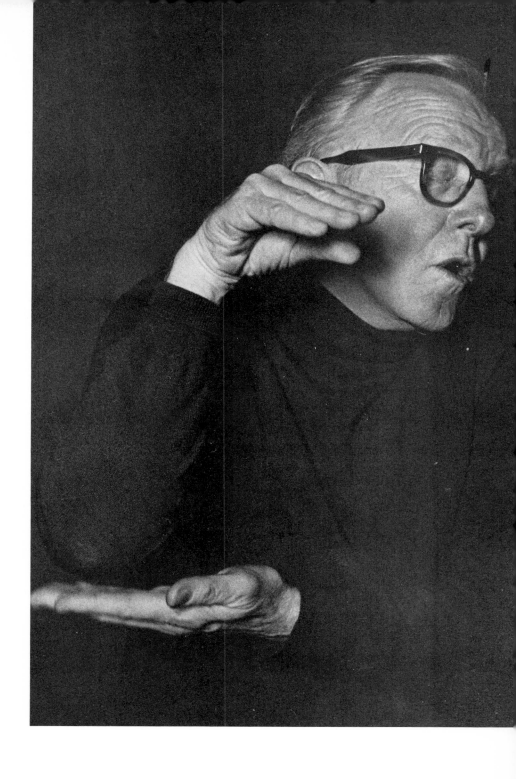

Ta gueule!—Your snout: Shut up!

Il a un poil dans la main!: He's lazy. The phrase means "He has a hair growing out of his hand," implying that his hand is not used much for work.

Il est bourré!—He's stuffed: He's potted; he's drunk.

Ça t'a passé sous le nez!—That passed under your nose: You missed your opportunity.

Les oeillères!—You're wearing blinders: Narrow-minded!

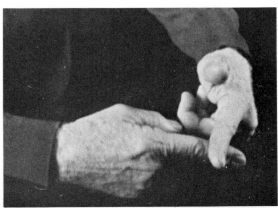

Je te donne ça, tu veux ça—I give you this, and you wish that: I give you an inch and you take a mile.

Two versions of ***Tu l'as dans le cul!***—You have it in your ass: You've let yourself be had!

C'est un cas!—He's a psychological case: He's nuts!

T'es toqué, non?!: You're nuts.

Mais qu'est-ce que tu as dans le crâne?!—But what is in
your skull?: Are you stupid?!

SEX

Sex

Il y a du monde au balcon!—There is a crowd in the balcony: What tits!

SEX

FOR A PEOPLE reputed to be absorbed with sex, this is a very short list of gestures related to it, and even these are not very sexy. They are also all gestures made by men, since the French women in our research group looked for gestures women might make and found none. Of course, I could lengthen the list by adding gestures relating to sexual organs, but they are not frequently used with implications of sexuality. *Il a du cul!,* for instance, certainly uses a sexual metaphor, but there is no sexual intention. The same may be said for *Le bras d'honneur!*

Pédé! is based on a play on words. The word is, of course, an abbreviation for "pederast," but it is represented by the little finger because *Pédé!* is pronounced like "p.d.," the initials of *petit doigt* ("little finger").

Men everywhere like to indicate the beauty of a woman's body through gesture. We could have used, for instance, the same gesture American men use to show that a woman is "well-stacked," but the image of *Il y a du monde au balcon!* seemed a more graphic and interesting choice. It may also be more French. I have no statistics to back up my opinion, but I believe that French women generally have smaller breasts than American women. Consequently, French men could be more interested in observing *le monde au balcon.*

Avoir du cul has nothing to do with the English idea of "a piece of ass." It refers literally to the ass and to the curious concept that a person who "has some ass" is lucky. It means the same as *avoir du pot* (*pot* means "pot," but here it is used in one of its slang meanings, "ass"). Perhaps this expression was im-

49

ported from Italy where *avere culo* means *essere fortunato,* "to be lucky."

Cocu!, which mimes horns, is an ancient gesture, as horns have been a symbol of power since the earliest times. The problem is how this symbol came also to represent the archetypal cuckold used by writers since the time of Greek comedies. The real explanation is lost in prehistory, so etymologists have been free to invent derivations. The most widely accepted etymology of the gesture is that the Greeks had a custom of grafting a capon's spurs onto his head, where they grew several inches in length. I am more attracted to the simpler explanation that extra horns are awarded to a weak husband to give him the power he should have to play his conventional role.

Cocu!—Cuckold!

Pédé!: Fairy!

Vous dansez?—Will you dance? The finger makes a circular, swirling motion, not indicated by the photograph.

52

Il a du cul!—He has some ass: He's really lucky!

AÏE! AÏE! AÏE!

Pain, Fright, and Surprise

OUCH!

WHY does a French child shake his fingers to express pain or the premonition of pain? I do not know whether this is a spontaneous body reaction or whether children learn the gesture through imitation of adults. In any case, to shake the hand so that the fingers flap together is the usual French expression for reaction to pain. It is the same hand motion we used in childhood to get the teacher to call on us, but in that gesture the arm was held straight over the head.

Non, mais je rêve! and *On a eu chaud!* are simple mimed gestures. One rubs the eyes to stimulate vision and to indicate that what one sees is so impossible that the eyes cannot be functioning properly. To have a narrow escape presumably makes one break out in a cold sweat, but, since sweating comes from heat, usually the expression for "that was a narrow one" becomes "we were hot." Then one mimes wiping off the sweat.

La trouille is a common expression meaning "fear." There is some question about its etymology, but the action of the gesture, indicating excretion, would seem to support the suggestion that the word comes from a Flemish word *drollen* meaning "to defecate."

Quelle horreur!—How awful!

Ça fait mal!—That hurts!

On a eu chaud!—We were hot: That was a narrow escape. "We were hot" is indicated by wiping away perspiration caused by fright.

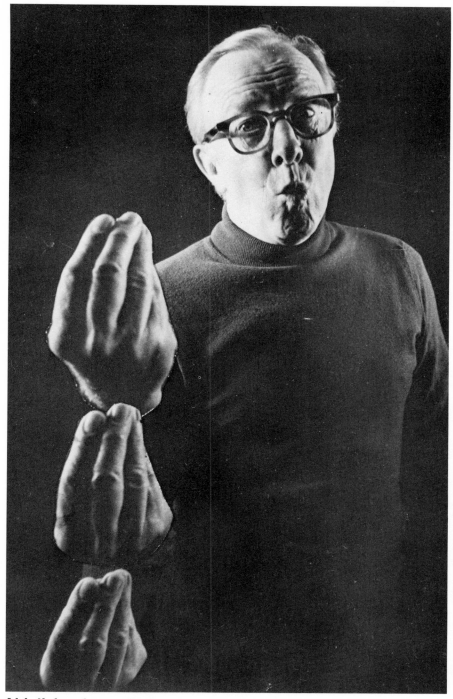

Ah! J'ai eu la trouille!—I had fright: I was really scared.

Non, mais je rêve!—No, but I'm dreaming!: I can't believe my eyes!

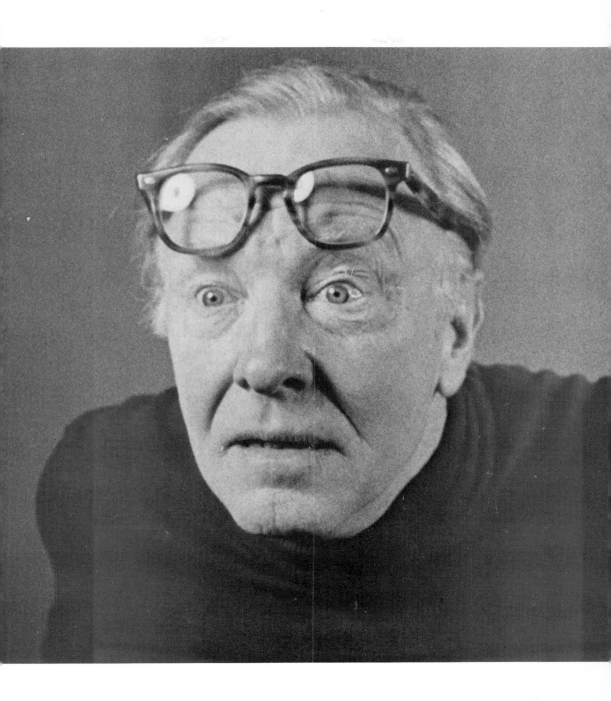

JEUX D'ENFANTS

Menace and Mockery
Among Children

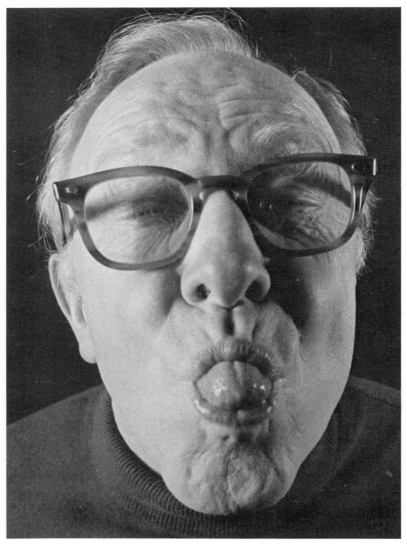

Je te tire la langue!—I stick my tongue out at you!

NYEH! NYEH! NYEH!

CHILDHOOD IS RICH with gesture, since communication with the whole body has not yet been suppressed. Children can be cruel, and most of these gestures call up the image of unkind, observing eyes focused on a victim—a child who has incurred disapproval. How typical is the schoolyard scene of a child surrounded by taunting hands and faces.

Les cornes! has a quite different meaning on the playground from the similar gesture referring to a man's marital situation. For adults "horns" suggests a man is a cuckold. For children *Les cornes!* refers to one's ears. Apparently, in the old days children who did not know their lessons were forced to wear a paper hat with long ears symbolizing a donkey's head. I have never witnessed this punishment, but even today children know the meaning of a *bonnet d'âne* ("cap of a donkey"), meaning "dunce's cap."

The derivation of the word *bisque!* is not clear, but the beard-pulling gesture shows that, at least in the popular mind, *bisque!* has become related to the word *bique,* which means "nanny goat." The main purpose of the gesture is to taunt a child who has displayed vexation and to make him even more miserable.

I used to pity the child in the Roussillon schoolyard on a cold winter morning when he had a runny nose. If he failed to wipe it he was soon surrounded by other children taunting, *"Chandelle! Chandelle!"* with the appropriate gesture.

Among the gestures adults make to children, perhaps the mildest is the finger shaking to accompany *Petit coquin.* If a child is seriously misbehaving, a stronger gesture and expression are used.

"You little rascal" has a tone of gentle scolding, even implying conniving approval of the child's mischief. The nagging index finger in *Pas de ça* is heeded as a more serious demand to stop an activity at once.

The threat to a child of *Tu veux une paire de baffes?!* seems curious. The French kiss on both cheeks too; do they perhaps have a compulsion to make symmetrical assaults on the face? Or does the slap with the back of the hand to one cheek imply that a child is rejected, while the slap with the palm on the other cheek, drawing the child closer, implies that the child is punished but still loved and accepted by the agent of punishment?

Left and Right: Different versions of ***Bisque, bisque, rage!***—Anger, anger, rage!: Goody, goody for you!

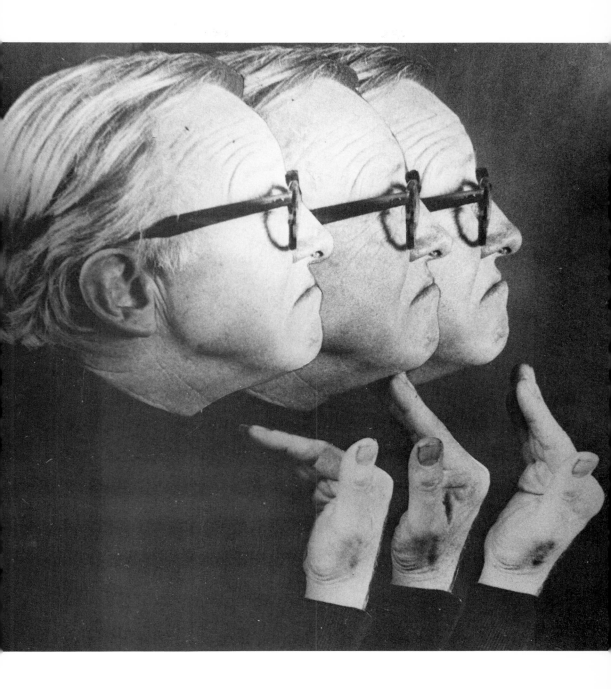

Chandelle!—Candle!: Wipe your runny nose! A runny nose is supposed to look like a dripping candle.

Hou! Les cornes!—Ha! The horns: You're a dunce with donkey's ears!

Tâte un peu!—Feel a little: Just feel that muscle!

Petit coquin!—You little rascal, you!

Pas de ça—Hey! None of that!

Tu veux une paire de baffes?!—You want a pair of slaps?: Stop that or I'll slap you. The word *baffe* is related to *bof.* The literal meaning suggests the sudden deflation of the cheeks brought about by the slaps.

FAIS GAFFE

Threat and Mayhem

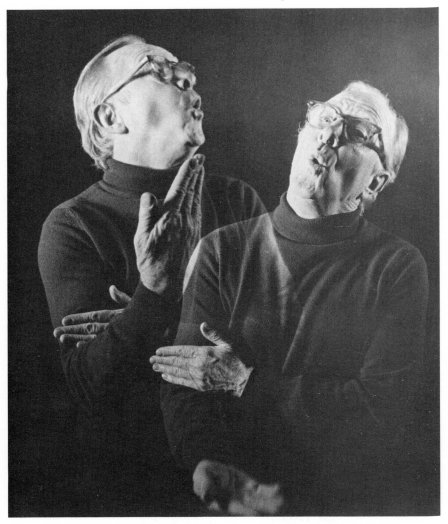

Va te faire foutre!—Go get yourself screwed!: The word *foutre* is used so often and in so many different ways in French that it is even less strong than the English "screw."

GO TO HELL!

WE HAVE SAVED the most violent gestures for the end and have placed them in ascending order of violence. *Le pied de nez,* which we have already discussed as the "Shanghai gesture," is fairly mild. It indicates a feeling of defiance, expressing delight in another person's discomfiture. The age of the gesture in French is indicated by the use of the word *pied.* Here it refers to an obsolete unit of measure, giving a whole foot of length to the other person's nose. "To have a long nose" (*avoir le nez long*) means to show a face indicating keen displeasure.

In *Va te faire foutre!* the gesture is not directly related to the words of the label. The action of raising the right arm with the hand tossing something over your shoulder or putting something behind you indicates utter disregard for the opinion of the other person. He can "go to hell," or in the French expression "go screw himself!" The gesture is strengthened sometimes by striking the right arm with the left hand, bringing in a shade of *Le bras d'honneur.* Or it can be combined with an expulsion of breath in the form of *Bof!* The head may even turn to the left at the same time to reinforce the feeling of ignoring the interlocutor.

With *Tu veux mon poing sur la gueule?* the threat becomes more serious. This one might have been included in the list of children's gestures since children frequently use the gesture without following up with violence. It indicates a stage of exasperation beyond that which may be relieved simply by oral aggression. However, among French adults who have been drilled in the art of aggression short of violence,

73

this threat is not so fearful as it might be among American men who are more likely to carry out their threats.

Finally, we come to the most insulting, the most violent, and the most infuriating of all gestures: *Le bras d'honneur,* known in English as the "Royal Shaft." Though this gesture is known in many countries, its home seems to be in the Mediterranean area. The Italians have developed many nuances, from tapping on the fingers to striking the nape of the neck with the left hand and extending the right arm full length. In any country in which you feel tempted to insult someone with this gesture, you should have your means of escape assured in advance.

Left and Right: Two versions of **_Le pied de nez_**—a nose
a foot long, with which one taunts the interlocutor.

Tu veux mon poing sur la gueule?!—Do you want my fist on your snout?: I'll knock your face in.

Le bras d'honneur!—The arm of honor: The Royal Shaft, the most *macho* of gestures. A man's honor is shown to reside in the strength of his arm and fist, here vaunted as a phallic symbol.

Index of Gestures